Welcome to Planet Reader!

Invite your child on a journey to a wonderful, imaginative place—
the limitless universe of reading! And there's no better traveling
companion than you, the parent. Every time you and your child read
together you send out an important message: Reading can be rewarding
and *fun*. This understanding is essential to helping your child build the
skills and confidence he or she needs as an emerging reader.

Here are some tips for sharing Planet Reader stories with your child:

Be open! Some children like to listen to or read the whole story and
then ask questions. Some children will stop on every page with a
question or a comment. Either way is fine; the most important thing
is that your child feels reading is a pleasurable experience.

Be understanding! Sometimes your child might need a direct answer.
If he or she points to a word and asks you to tell what it is, do so.
Other times, your child may want to sound out a word or stop to figure
out a sentence independently. Allow for both approaches.

Enjoy! The story and characters in this book were created especially for
your child's age group. Talk about the story. Take turns reading favorite
parts. Look at how the illustrations support the story and enhance the
reading experience.

And most of all, enjoy your child's journey into literacy. It's one of the
most important trips the two of you will ever take!

To Joan Bowden, who always believed in this story;

to Ann Tanner, whose friend told me about the flood;

and to Maggie Dahms, for her friendship and her name.

B. W. B.

To Luke, who should be entering the world at about

the time this book is published. God bless you!

J. L.

Wm
L.
Lic
Brus
12.95

THE Great Molasses Flood

by Beth Wagner Brust

illustrated by John Lund

Troll

Maggie Malone wanted something exciting to happen *every* day. But everyday life is not always exciting. So Maggie made things up.

"I saw elves today! A dozen of them! They danced up Copp's Hill," she told old Mr. Vanelli.

He rolled his eyes and kept watering his plants.

"Ma, I saw mermaids! They were swimming in Boston Harbor."

Maggie's mother shook her head and kept peeling potatoes.

"I saw Paul Revere's ghost," Maggie told the local fire chief. "He galloped down the street. He was shouting, 'The British are coming! The British are coming!' It sounded like the start of the Revolutionary War!"

The chief laughed. He jumped two of her checkers.

Then, on January 15, 1919, everything changed. It was warm for a winter day. Maggie sat on the deck of Fireboat No. 31 with her father. She had brought him lunch. She liked coming to the harbor. She liked walking past the big buildings. She liked walking under the huge tank. Her father said it held more than two million gallons of molasses.

Life seemed more exciting down
at the harbor.

"Now off with you, Maggie, darling,"
said her father. He wiped his mouth.
"I've got work to do. No playing about
on the way home."

"Aw, Pa, let me stay!" Maggie begged.

"No, you skedaddle," he said. He
handed her the lunch basket. He led her
up the ramp.

Maggie strolled down the street. She
stopped to take off her sweater. She
looked up at the huge steel tank
full of molasses.

It was as wide as three houses. It
was as tall as a five-story clock tower.

Maggie swung on its thick steel
beams. Up and down. Up and down.

She crossed the street. Maggie
heard the clickety-clack of the trolley
overhead. She swung her basket in
time with the sound. Up and down.
Up and down.

Then Maggie heard a strange noise.

RAT-A-TAT-TAT.

She looked up. The trolley was gone.

She heard the sound again. It was louder this time.

RAT-A-TAT-TAT.

Maggie looked behind her.

All she saw were some horses pulling a wagon. Then she heard a BIG noise. Like a million firecrackers going off!

RAT-A-TAT-TAT-TAT-TAT-TAT-TAT-TAT-TAT-TAT-TAT.

It made her jump.

Maggie dropped her basket. She ran behind a lamppost.

Metal bolts zinged by. They landed all around her.

KA-BOOM! A huge piece of steel flew past her. A sweet-sour smell filled the air.

Maggie peeked around the pole.
She gasped! There was a huge hole
in the big tank. Great globs of
molasses gushed out.

17

Molasses flowed *fast* down the street in a large, dark wave. Horses galloped hard to run from it. The wall of molasses was four times as tall as Maggie. A flower cart, a street bench, and a bicycle tumbled on top of the wave.

It was heading right for her!

Maggie wanted to run to her father. But the molasses was in the way. So she ran to the nearest house. She pounded on the door.

"Help!" she shouted. "Call someone! The molasses is coming! The molasses is coming!"

Old Mr. Vanelli looked down from the second floor.

"Maggie Malone, is that you? Santa Maria, why do you bother me with another crazy story?"

Maggie watched the tall, dark wave of molasses rolling toward her.

"I'm telling the truth," she cried. "Just look up the street!" And away she ran.

Mr. Vanelli shook his head. Then he looked over and saw the wall of molasses.

"*Aieeee!* She's right!" he said.

Maggie ran down the street. "Help! Help!" she yelled. "The molasses is coming! The molasses is coming!"

She looked back. The dark brown wave was three times as tall as Maggie. It had a scooter, a mailbox, and a barrel of apples riding in the swell.

At the top tumbled Maggie's basket!

Maggie reached her house and threw open the door. Her mother was in the parlor. She was serving tea to her friends.

"Help, Ma, help!" Maggie shouted. "The molasses is coming! The molasses is coming! Call somebody!"

The ladies looked shocked. Her mother sighed.

"Ladies, this is Mary Margaret. She likes to make up stories."

Maggie waved her arms. "This is not a story, Ma! In a few minutes, you'll all be up to your ankles in molasses!"

Maggie rushed to the door. "I have to find out if Pa is all right." And away she ran.

Her mother looked out the window. The big wave of molasses was a few houses away.

"Glory be! Maggie's right," she said. She fell into a chair and fainted.

Maggie ran to the fire station. She rang the bell.

Clang! Clang! Clang!

Firemen slid down the pole. They stopped when they saw Maggie.

"Jeepers, it's only you," one said.

"Hurry," begged Maggie. "The molasses is coming! The molasses is coming! You've got to stop it."

The fire chief pointed at her. "Maggie Malone," he said. "You know better than to sound a fire alarm when there is no fire."

"There may not be a fire," she told him. "But there is molasses. Millions of gallons of it! Look!"

Now the wave of molasses was about Maggie's height. It rolled straight toward them. A street sign, a window box, and a doghouse tumbled in its swell.

Jumping and barking at the wave was a little dog. The dog wanted its house back.

"Gadzooks!" shouted the fire captain. "Grab the hoses, men! Let's turn the flood toward the harbor."

The crew held firehoses. They blasted water on the molasses. The water pushed the brown ooze toward the docks.

Maggie started a bucket brigade with other children. They scooped water from the harbor.

Maggie poured buckets of saltwater on the molasses. She noticed something.

"Chief, look!" said Maggie.

She poured the saltwater on the molasses. The molasses melted!

The fire chief called all fireboats to
come to the North End. He wanted
them to spray saltwater on the thick,
gooey molasses. It would help clean off
the sticky streets.

"What about my pa?" asked Maggie. "Is he coming?"

"I don't know," said the fire chief. "We'll see who shows up."

They waited and waited. Finally,
a fireboat pulled up. It was Maggie's
father!

"Oh, Pa, you're okay," cried Maggie. She ran into his arms. She gave him a big, sticky hug.

"Barely, darling," he said. "When the tank broke open, it crushed the station. We were lucky that it missed our boat."

He gave her a squeeze. "I heard you were just like Paul Revere. You warned everyone."

"I tried!" said Maggie. "But no one would believe me."

Her father laughed. "Maggie, darling, how can you blame them? You do come out with some mighty big tales!"

Maggie looked at the river of molasses. She said nothing.

From that day on, Maggie Malone
did not make up as many wild stories.
After all, what could be as wild as what
really happened on that warm winter
day in Boston?

Author's Note

Over two million gallons of molasses spilled in the Great Molasses Flood of 1919. The tank was not strong enough to hold so much weight.

It took people living in the North End many months to recover. They scraped and scrubbed the sticky brown molasses off their houses, shops, and streets.

And even now, on a hot summer day, people say that you can still smell a hint of molasses on the streets in the North End of Boston.

About the Author

Born and raised in southern California, Beth Wagner Brust moved east after college to see what the other coast of America was like. For four years she lived in Washington, D.C., and that's where she first heard about the Great Molasses Flood. It sounded so incredible, she had to write about it!

Ms. Brust is the author of the award-winning book *The Amazing Paper Cuttings of Hans Christian Andersen*. She has also written seven Zoobooks and a trio of easy readers.

Ms. Brust lives in San Diego with her surfing scientist husband and two young sons.

About the Illustrator

After years of circling the globe chasing rainbows, John Lund finally embarked on a career as a children's book illustrator. Being mainly self-taught, he challenged himself to study various styles of art, ranging from realism to cartoons. He has illustrated books in The Wubbulous World of Dr. Seuss and Sesame Street series.

Mr. Lund lives in Vancouver, Canada.